For Mom, who taught me to read the water,
and for Dad, who taught me to read the wind
-MF

For my Lydia—may you always find seas of imagination to explore,
inspired stories to share, a true friend to join the adventure,
and joyful love to fill the sails of your heart.
Forever your talking buddy
-LF

little bee books

An imprint of Bonnier Publishing USA
251 Park Avenue South, New York, NY 10010
Text copyright © 2018 by Meg Fleming
Illustrations copyright © 2018 by Luke Flowers
All rights reserved, including the right of reproduction in whole or in part in any form.
Little Bee Books is a trademark of Bonnier Publishing USA, and associated
colophon is a trademark of Bonnier Publishing USA.
Manufactured in China   HH 1217
First Edition   10 9 8 7 6 5 4 3 2 1
ISBN 978-1-4998-0533-8
Library of Congress Cataloging-in-Publication Data
Names: Fleming, Meg, author. | Flowers, Luke, illustrator.
Title: Ready, Set, Sail! / by Meg Fleming; illustrated by Luke Flowers.
Description: First edition. | New York, NY: Little Bee Books, [2018]
Summary: Follows a group of friends as they go sailing, explore an island,
and return home to tell their tale. | Identifiers: LCCN 2017003452
Subjects: | CYAC: Stories in rhyme. | Sailing—Fiction. | Friendship—Fiction.
Classification: LCC PZ8.3.F639 Rh 2018 | DDC [E]—dc23
LC record available at https://lccn.loc.gov/2017003452

littlebeebooks.com
bonnierpublishingusa.com

READY, SET, SAIL!

words by
Meg Fleming

pictures by
Luke Flowers

 little bee books

Grab your life vest. Zip that zipper.

Throw the bowline to your skipper.

Keep your compass close at hand.

Shove away from rock and sand.

Row the dinghy to your boat.
Work together. Stay afloat.

Shout your orders loud and fast.
"Hoist the mainsail up the mast!"

Wind starts puffing. Don't delay.

Rudder ready?

"Anchors aweigh!"

Mainsheet flutters. Catch that gale.
Want it faster? Trim the sail!

Speeding. Slipping. Leaning. Tipping.

Perfect time for tiptoe dipping.

Find an island. Dive. Explore.

Someone's spouting near the shore!

Sails are calling. Lines are free.
Find the wind. Know the sea.

LUXOWE

Mind the traffic. Go or stay?
Sailboats get the right-of-way.

HAPPY
SNAPPER
CRAB CO.

Winds of change may slow your zoom.

Watch that boom!

Ducking heads and switching places.
Salty mist on homeward faces.

Catch your buoy. Anchor down.

Tie things up and head to town.

Time to tell about that whale.

Every sailor has a tale!